Dr. H Explores the Universe
©Unapologetically Being, Inc. 2018-Present

Illustrator Patrick Giles

Published in the United States of America

Unapologetically Being, Inc.
3157 Gentilly Blvd #2029
New Orleans, LA 70122
985-236-1913

Website: www.drhexplores.com
Email: Contact@drhexplores.com

Hardback ISBN 978-0-9993512-8-4 Published 2021
Paperback ISBN 978-0-9993512-7-7 Published 2023

This book series is dedicated to changing the face of Science, Technology, Engineering and Math one story at a time.

Dedicated to Dayten and Gabriel, who will live out my legacy and to my godchildren Terrell, Asyia, Christian and Aurell Renee who love me just because.

Thank you Eric, Malik, and Denise for your support and living in my legacy. Thank you to my parents for doing what you did to make me who I am. Thank you to everyone who has supported what we believe in by purchasing the books and other items.

-K. Renee

EXPLORES THE MOON
Dr. H

Author: K Renee Horton, Ph.D

Artist: Patrick Giles

A storm was brewing outside as BB sat on the side of the street. His windshield wipers zipped back and forth as he stared up at the nasty clouds. The rain would make him clean and shiny, but BB still didn't want to sit out in the storm. He was about to get some shuteye when he spotted Dr.H rushing out of her house.

BB popped open the driver's side door as Dr. H jumped inside. He couldn't help but giggle at her drenched appearance. Dr. H huffed as she peered out the rain covered windshield. Even with his windshield wipers going full blast, Dr. H couldn't see anything further than BB's headlights.

"It's been raining all day long, and I have had quite enough," Dr. H muttered, as BB grew excited. Whenever she was fed up with something on Earth, she and BB would always venture up into space. He waited with anticipation to see where they were headed today. "We're going to the Moon!"

But before BB could zoom up into the clouds, he spotted someone else running out of Dr. H's home. It was Kevin, her lab assistant, and friend. He was dragging Dr. H's spacesuit as he tried not to trip on it. BB popped open his trunk and Kevin folded the suit inside. He ran to the driver's side window as Dr. H rolled it down.

"Thank you for remembering my suit, Kevin. You're an absolute lifesaver," Dr. H said as the pair hive-fived.

"You're very welcome, Dr. H. You two be careful heading into space today. The weather down here is awful," Kevin warned them before stepping back.

Dr. H and BB promised they would be safe and careful, and then they sped into the cloudy sky. Kevin waved to them until they vanished into the thick, grey clouds. BB realized right away, why Kevin had told them to be careful. The heavy clouds and rain created a very unsteady ride.

"It's okay, BB. That's just turbulence caused by the storm. Everything will be okay."

And sure enough, they broke through the clouds and carried on flying with ease without any more turbulence. Like always, space was quiet and vast, and it was just the way they liked it. BB set a course for the moon and traveled through space as fast as his purple body could move.

"How far away is the moon, Dr. H?"

"It's 384,400 km away, which means it would take us around six months to drive there normally," Dr. H explained. "Lucky for us, you're a special vehicle."

He truly was special, because it only took them about a half hour to reach the moon. But as they approached the moon, BB noticed something odd about its shape.

"Um, Dr. H? Is this the right moon?"

"Yes, it is. Why do you ask?"

"Because it doesn't look very circular to me. All the pictures show the Earth's moon as circular," BB said.

"Although photos show the moon as a circle, it's actually a bit more egg-shaped because of its rotation," Dr. H explained.

BB was surprised to learn that fact. As they flew in a circle around the moon, he could clearly see the oval shape. As BB flew down for landing, Dr. H explained that the first ever spaceship to reach the moon had been Russia's Luna 1. It was all the way back in 1959, but they never landed on the moon.

That honor was left to the American astronaut Neil Armstrong, who was the first to step foot on the moon. Now, it was BB and Dr.H's turn to land. Dr. H slipped into the backseat and retrieved her spacesuit from the trunk. She hopped out when she was ready.

BB was surprised that he and Dr. H seemingly bounced on the surface of the moon. Dr. H explained that gravity is, weaker on the moon because of how much smaller its mass was. A person or magic vehicle would only weigh one-sixth of what they would weigh on Earth. The purple beetle took advantage of that by bouncing all around.

Dr. H jumped around, and then slowly returned to the ground, only to jump again. BB had uncovered a crater or hole in the moon's surface. He sped into the hole and flew into the sky on the other side. BB came to a stop in front of another big hole.

"Dr. H, why are there so many holes on the moon's surface?"

"The holes are called impact craters. They formed when meteors hit the surface throughout the centuries. Asteroids have also collided with the moon's surface."

BB was shocked to learn that all those holes were from objects impacting the moon. They must have been large asteroids and meteors to make such deep holes. The pair continued to explore the moon when he had another pesky question. BB had no idea why the moon was so important.

"The high and low tides we experience on Earth are caused by the moon's gravitational pull. Without the moon, our tides and Earth's rotation would be impacted poorly. The planet would be so wobbly!" exclaimed Dr. H.

Dr. H gave BB specific directions but wouldn't say where they were driving. She sat on his roof as BB bounced his way to her secret destination. When they arrived, BB was amazed to see a massive and tall mountain.

"This is Mons Huygens. It is the tallest mountain on the moon," Dr. H said. "It stands an impressive 5.5 kilometers high."

"That's really tall," BB said.

"Dr. H, I read somewhere that there's a dark side to the moon, but we haven't come across it yet. Is there really a dark side?" BB asked as he began to climb the mountain but decided against it.

"The dark side is actually a myth. The side we see on Earth is called the near side. The side we don't see is called the far side. However, both sides are lit evenly by the sun."

"Oh, that makes sense. I thought that phrase sounded a bit silly."

Just then, a tiny screen on Dr. H's sleeve lit up with Kevin's face. The suit came with a screen that connected her with Earth in case she ever had an emergency.

"Hi, Kevin. Do you need something?"

"Hi, Kevin!" BB screamed as he flashed his lights.

"Hi, guys! I just wanted to warn you that nighttime is approaching. You don't want to be caught on the moon when it's night," Kevin warned the pair of explorers. "Also, the storm has subsided down here, so you're clear for landing."

"Thanks for the heads up, Kevin. We'll make our way back now," Dr. H said and turned off the live feed to Earth. "Well, looks like our adventure is over for the day."

"What will happen if we stay on the moon during the night? Do nighttime monsters live on the moon?!" BB screeched, suddenly terrified.

"Don't worry, BB. There are no monsters on the moon. We shouldn't remain on the moon after dark because it grows quite cold. It can drop down to -153 degrees Celsius!"

That was all BB had to hear. He popped open the driver's side door as Dr.H. giggled and entered.

He didn't feel like freezing tonight, so he was fine with returning home. Dr.H. slipped out of her spacesuit and snuggled in for the drive home. She watched the moon slowly shrink as BB began to contemplate what their next adventure would be. Would it be another planet or maybe another moon? He was excited to find out.

The end, until the next adventure.

Discussion Questions
Theresa Apodaca, the 2009 New Mexico Academy of Sciences
Science Teacher of the Year.

1. As BB is waiting for Dr. H he notices a storm brewing. What does brewing mean in this sentence? Draw a picture of a storm brewing. Write a caption for your picture using descriptive sentences.

2. When BB and Dr. H sped into the cloudy sky, the clouds were thick and grey. What is another way to spell the color grey? As BB and Dr. H continued into the heavy clouds and rain, the ride became unsteady. Dr. H told BB that it's okay because "it's just turbulence". What does turbulence mean? Write five sentences that include the word turbulence.

3. On their way to the Moon BB asked Dr. H, "How far away is the moon?" Dr. H told BB it is 384,400 km away. How many miles would that be? If you don't know how to convert kilometers (km) to miles, use the following example. Imagine that you're being asked to convert 7 kilometers into miles. There are 0.6214 kilometers in 1 mile, now all you have to do is fill the numbers into the conversion formula and multiply: ? kilometers × 0.6214 = ? miles
7 kilometers × 0.6214 = 4.3498 miles
As they continued on their adventure, BB was amazed to see a massive and tall mountain. Dr. H said, "This is Mons Huygens and it is the tallest mountain on the Moon. It stands 5.5 kilometers high". How tall is the mountain in miles? In feet? (Hint: there are 5280 feet in 1 mile.)

Compare it to the tallest mountain on Earth, Mount Everest. Which mountain is tallest? Create a bar graph showing the heights in kilometers, miles and feet.

4. BB was surprised to find out that the Moon was oval instead of round shaped. Dr. H said it is because of its rotation. How long does it take the Moon to rotate on its axis? Another way to ask, how many Earth days does it take for the Moon to rotate on its axis? Hint: this is also the amount of time it takes for the Moon to complete its orbit around Earth. "lunar cycle calendar". What does this have to do with "the dark side of the moon"?

5. The Moon not only rotates on its axis, but it also revolves around Earth while doing so. As the Moon rotates and revolves around Earth, it goes through different lunar phases as can be seen from Earth. Explain what this means. Write a descriptive paragraph and draw the lunar cycles. You can find what the phases of the moon are by doing a word search on "lunar cycle calendar". What does this have to do with "the dark side of the moon"?

6. On July 16, 1969, astronauts Neil Armstrong, Edwin "Buzz" Aldrin, and Michael Collins began their historic voyage to the Moon and back. The Apollo 11 mission had three spacecraft: the Command Module Columbia, a Service Module, and the Lunar Module Eagle. Describe how each spacecraft was used for this mission.

Explain how the astronauts were able to land on the Moon and later back to the command module. When Apollo 11 astronaut Neil Armstrong stepped on the surface of the Moon he said "That's one small step for man; one giant leap for mankind." What does this mean to you? How long were the astronauts on the Moon? What data did they collect while on the Moon? When did the astronauts get back to Earth?

7. Dr. H explained to BB they could bounce on the surface of the Moon because it has a smaller mass than Earth's causing weaker gravity. Compare the masses of Earth and the Moon using a bar graph. What math problems can you come up with from analyzing the graph? Dr. H also told BB that a person or object weighs only one-sixth of what they would weigh on Earth (because of the weaker gravity and smaller mass). If BB weighs about 1900 pounds on Earth, how much would the purple beetle weigh on the Moon? Hint: multiply 1900 pounds by the Moon's gravity relative to Earth's, which is 0.165.

8. BB noticed that the surface of the Moon has many holes and Dr. H explains that they are impact craters. What's the difference between comets, asteroids, meteoroids, meteors and meteorites? The moon has many craters; research at least five prominent craters on the near side of the Moon; include their locations and diameters.

Graph the diameters to compare sizes. Write an analysis of the results that the graph shows.

9. As Dr. H and BB continued exploring the Moon, BB wondered why the Moon is so important. Dr. H told BB that the high and low tides we experience on Earth are caused by the Moon's gravitational pull. Where do high and low tides happen on Earth? Explain what happens to the water at low tide.

Explain what happens to the water at high tide. If you are in Wellfleet, Massachusetts how will you know when high tide and low tide happen? Why would you even want to know this information?

10. Towards the end of their adventure Kevin warns Dr. H and BB that nighttime is approaching on the Moon and they should make their way back to Earth. BB asked Dr. H what would happen if they spent the night on the Moon. Dr. H explained that the temperature can be quite cold and drop down to -153° Celsius. What would the night temperature be in degrees Fahrenheit? Hint: use this formula to convert: F =1.8 x C+ 32.

What are the temperatures (both Celsius and Fahrenheit) during the day on the Moon? How did the lunar astronauts Neil Armstrong, Edwin "Buzz" Aldrin, and Michael Collins survive the extreme temperatures on the Moon?

www.ingramcontent.com/pod-product-compliance
Lightning Source LLC
Chambersburg PA
CBHW041130100726
47911CB00002B/89